TAKING CARE OF MOM

BY GINA AND MERCER MAYER

A GOLDEN BOOK • NEW YORK

 Published in the United States by Golden Books, an imprint of Random House Children's Books, a division of Penguin Random House LLC, 1745 Broadway, New York, NY 10019, and in Canada by Penguin Random House Canada Limited, Toronto. Originally published by Golden Books in 1993.
rhcbooks.com • littlecritter.com
Educators and librarians, for a variety of teaching tools, visit us at RHTeachersLibrarians.com
ISBN 978-1-9848-3089-0 (trade) — ISBN 978-1-9848-3090-6 (ebook)
Printed in the United States of America
10 9 8 7 6 5 4 3 2 1

Mom was sick. She had a stuffy nose and a fever.

She had to stay in bed all day. She couldn't even take us to the playground.

Dad had to go to work, so Grandma came to pick up my baby brother.

Grandma said my sister and I should go to her house, too.

But we didn't want to. We wanted to stay home to take care of Mom.

Grandma said, "All right, but you have to let your mother rest."

We were really careful not to bother Mom.

We got dressed by ourselves.

We fixed our own breakfast.

I found my favorite game
without asking for help.

I even opened a bag of chips by myself.

We only bothered Mom when it was really important—like when my sister spilled the jar of pickles.

We took Mom some juice when we thought she might be thirsty. We only spilled a little bit on her bed.

We fixed Mom a sandwich for lunch.

We didn't know what kind she would want, so we put a little of everything on it.

We tried to keep the puppy off her bed. He sure was sneaky, though.

We took my mom
a hot water bottle to
keep her warm. But it
leaked a little.

And we brought her another box of tissues. Her nose was so red.

We even cleaned up a little bit.

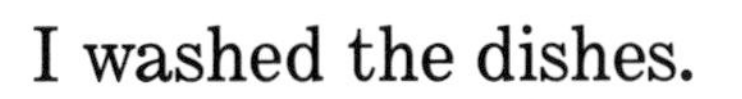

I washed the dishes.

My sister picked up some of the toys.

Then we decided to go outside to play. We put on our own coats and hats.

We told Mom we would be outside in case she needed us.

We played outside all afternoon.

When we came back in, Mom looked like she was feeling a little better.

Mom was better because we took such good care of her. Dad said he thought so, too.

Taking care of Mom was fun.

But I like it a lot better
when she takes care of us.